Face the Wind

An Exceptional American Story

KEN BARBER

Illustration by Luke Langley
Cover Design by Kevin O'Conner

ISBN: 148397183X
ISBN-13: 978-1483971834

TO MY CHILDREN,
AND MY CHILDREN'S
CHILDREN.

ACKNOWLEDGEMENTS

Having exhibited the traits and virtues of the characters in *Face the Wind*—sometimes all of them in a single day—I remain indebted and very grateful to everyone who has touched my life. I tried to thank you along the way.

However, I would especially like to thank Mum and Dad, who showed me and my two brothers, Mike and Nick, what togetherness really means. My ongoing thanks go to Candace, for not just putting up with, but managing to love a very strange bird, and to our children—Carina, Bethanie, David, Grace, Abigail, and Natalie—who have always given me something to live for, and something to smile about. To Dr. McDaniels and his team, who gave me something to smile with: Thanks, Mark; you are the epitome of the American gentleman that Charles Dickens so admired.

To the many people who have endured with me, especially Rosemary Lambert—you are such a quiet and faithful friend to many—and, in order of appearance: Gerry Watts, who soldiers on back in the UK; and John Bailey, Neil Allen and Stan Reed, a true band of brothers. To all those on the 102 who shared in my commute, and to the many kind people at 5th & Olive who encouraged me, thanks for being my focus group; and to Mark Endzell and Doug Wolfe, thanks for being so gracious while it incubated.

Finally, Jen and Connie, you rock.

Ken Barber
Seattle, Washington, USA
2013

CHAPTER ONE: A NAME YOU CAN LIVE WITH

"Dad, how did I get my name?" blurted out the young bird. "I mean nobody else in the coop has it."

Bantam, with the trained eye of an ex-fighting cock, measured his son, and if beaks could bend you would have detected a wry smile. "Well, let me see now, we always believed that if you were old enough to ask a question you were old enough to hear the truth. So . . ." and pausing as he looked up he asked, "what do you see up there?"

Knowing that Bantam never wasted his breath by asking idle questions the youngster, peering intently, followed his father's gaze into an almost clear blue sky. With a superior vision, which he had learned to keep a well-guarded secret, he easily identified the unmistakable profiles of a handful of seagulls. "Why, gulls." he replied.

"Yep," affirmed Bantam, "the depositors of doo-doo from on high, the defecators of doom, the stukas of stool, the showerers of . . ." and as he rattled off a heartfelt and well-practiced litany of alliteration on the frequency and carelessness of the bowel movements of seagulls, he simultaneously and almost subconsciously maneuvered himself until he stood only a couple of paces in front of his son. This was a tacit but clear signal that a subject of some importance had been broached and that it was about to be seriously addressed.

"Well, you've probably figured that you ain't no chicken . . ." and the rooster paused, ensuring that his observation had not overly disturbed the young bird. " . . . At least no chicken that I've ever seen, and I can't rightly say what you are even now, much less back then . . ." his voice had dropped momentarily into a wistful tone as he recalled, "I never saw Ma Bantam ever deny help to anyone," and then catching himself on the verge of a sigh the older bird cleared his throat and continued, " . . . so it didn't surprise me that the farmer, like he'd done a few times before, slipped an egg under her one morning.

"But this particular egg had you inside, and like everything about you it was different—and it was big! To this day I can't rightly recall everything and exactly what he said, but I do remember this much, he definitely said that your egg was 'an E. Gull's egg,' and though I didn't know what the *E* stood for, I knew this much—chickens hate gulls. In fact, they dislike just about anything that isn't a chicken, especially if it's big, and especially if it can fly, and it sure doesn't help if it poops on them. Chickens also turn nasty real quick, especially if what riles them is an easy target, like a chick or an egg. So it seemed to fit, and it appealed to my sense of the ironic to think that the *E* in 'E. Gull' might stand for *Enormous* and that I should call you Norm, for short. 'Cuz normal you ain't!"

Resisting the impulse to cackle, the rooster quickly and softly added, "Leastwise, I figured it was a name that wouldn't get you killed."

"So, do you think I'm a gull, Pa?"

"Nope, not really. You don't much resemble a gull. In fact, the closest thing I've ever seen that looks like you is called a hawk, and I've seen a few of them, but they were all way tinier than you, and I don't believe you're even full grown yet. Also, gulls and hawks can fly, and when I say hawks can fly I mean they can really fly, but with that big body of yours, not to mention those tree-trunk legs, you ain't ever gettin' off the ground!"

Bantam, recalling his earlier rant against gulls, gently concluded their conversation with an encouraging and familiar exhortation, "Son, you've also got a big heart, and you're bright so you ask a lot of good questions, but we don't always get all the answers in this life and when we do get them they often come in the strangest ways. However, there is a reason for everything and a purpose for everyone, eventually the truth will reveal itself. In the meantime, remember, whatever you are and whatever they do, you've got to love those chickens."

CHAPTER TWO: PECKING ORDER

The chickens in the coop that Norm lived in were divided into three grades, the boundaries of which were never crossed. To do so would have violated the revered and time-honored cornerstone of chickendom, that most sacred of all observances—tradition. It would also have been a suicidal breach of the coopocracy. (Some still whispered, however, that before the establishment of order, the chickens once ran wild and free, and that originally the coop had actually been founded as a co-op. Although few recognized the importance of the distinction between the two terms.)

Atop the coop were the Ruesters, all of them Rhode Island Reds who, strangely enough, were actually predominantly white. Haughty, proud, and aloof, their singular task was to rule the roost, an undertaking that they conducted with considerable dignity. Had they not wielded their authority with such severity, and had they not taken themselves quite so seriously, they might have been considered quite noble creatures.

The Ruesters are governed by Garic, the head Ruester, who presides over the coop with unquestioned authority. He alone is vested with the singularly important and vital task of alerting everyone to the daily surprise of sunrise. His dominance over the other Ruesters and their collective supremacy over the coop, with the benign support of the Friars, and the later insidious, ever-expanding, and pervasive assistance of the Süds, was unchallenged and absolute—that is, except for the notable and infuriating exception of Bantam, and the growing and awkwardly ill-defined threat of his young protégé.

The Friars, whose designation as *fryers* was corrupted, as designations frequently are, by the capitalizing on and misappropriation of their calling, had drab brownish-black plumage and were afforded the full freedom of the coop. Most of the Friars possessed a detached air, but all of them, on a seemingly voluntary basis, dutifully helped with the indoctrination and promotion of the religious, moral, and historical culture and beliefs of the flock and reported any deviance from its orthodoxy to the Ruesters. This made for a mutually beneficial and protective relationship that helped to maintain the Ruesters and the Friars in their elevated status above the flock.

Although the Friars were never under constraint to do much of anything, they, like the Süds, were pointedly never neglected in the daily feeding. Coop protocol mandated that after the Ruesters had eaten their fill, the Friars, who, although they only comprised a small fraction of the flock, took one tenth of what remained. Additionally, in the days that immediately preceded the fulfillment of their mysterious calling, great care was taken by the humans to ensure that one of the Friars was lavishly and profusely fed. Almost unfailingly, every week, one of them would receive the ultimate call for a Friar, an invitation, sometimes even spoken aloud by the farmer, to come to the farmhouse for Sunday dinner! This was a sacred, albeit nervously anticipated honor, as none of the flock quite understood what exactly happened to the chosen guest after the ritual carrying away by the farmer from the coop to the barn for what was in hushed and reverential tones referred to as the Sabbatical Initiation Ceremony.

One thing was for sure, once chosen, no Friars ever came back to the coop, which perturbed no one unduly, as chickens, their short memories and even shorter attention spans, having been further blunted by the rigors and monotony of coop life, generally and casually accepted that they must have gone to a much better place.

Finally came the lowest class of chickens, the lay-chickens. They supplied the eggs which the farmer and his family gathered so carefully every late afternoon. Great importance was attached to these eggs, and those chickens that produced the most were usually rewarded with preferred positions in their roosts. Occasionally, but obviously for some well-warranted reason, the farmer would accord a delighted lay-chicken the privilege of hatching one or even several of her eggs, a distinction which provoked both affection for, and jealousy against, the honoree and her brood from the other lay-chickens. This ambivalence betrayed the still-fertile and yet brutally calloused emotions of those that had become accustomed but not yet quite fully resigned to the routine removal of embryonic promise.

The lay-chickens, unlike the Ruesters and the Friars, came in every variety of shape, size, and color and made up the vast majority of the coop. They lived and slept in one of the fifty state-of-the-art henhouses, which in the early days of the farm (and way before the sinister advent of the Süds) had originally been thirteen henhouses, each of which was governed by a rooster with the aid of an attendant Friar or two, who, back then, actually lived with and among their respective broods. In those days each rooster, representing their henhouse, convened with the other roosters to negotiate and agree on basic rules of conduct and on their common defense against invading critters. Then they would return to their houses, and with the aid of the resident Friars, apply the observance of these agreed on and foundational rules in a manner that brought the greatest harmony to the entire flock and yet upheld the unique values and state of their homes.

However, the farm experienced a time of prosperity and rapid growth and, seemingly in the name of reason and efficiency, these familiar ties were broken as almost all of the Ruesters and Friars (and all of the ubiquitous and interloping Süds) now lived and slept in the centrally located henhouse, named The Great Congress, from which were dispensed the collective dictates of the Ruesters.

CHAPTER THREE:
HOW TO PLAY CHICKEN

Most of the days in the coop were pretty uneventful, some pleasantly so and most tediously so, but this, evidently, was not going to be one of them. There were ritual sacrifices that occurred with unnerving and erratic frequency. Sometimes they apparently happened spontaneously but on other occasions they climaxed a season of underlying but increasing tension. Whenever or however they came about the result was always the same—the status quo of the coop was brutally reinforced.

Norm, paralyzed and sickened with fear, watched with mounting horror as a number of chickens began to form a circle around an aggrieved Ruester and a helpless chick and its terrified but protective mother. What was coming next was inevitable. Perhaps the chick had done something wrong, like defecating on the public highways between the coops, a privilege reserved only for Ruesters, who were never to be distracted from the much more urgent and important matters that constantly preoccupied them. Probably the chick had done nothing wrong at all, because what really mattered was that somebody's agenda or advances had been opposed or rejected. When the wrong Ruester took offence a killing was coming.

Soon his murderous beak would make its initial strike and, even if the kill were quick and sure, a riot would ensue. The sight of blood, the flurry of feathers, and the plaintive and futile cries for mercy incited the flock to rush upon and silence the condemned, pecking furiously as they simultaneously evidenced their submission to, and vented their frustration at, the hierarchy of the coop. Flying beads of blood excited fresh attacks on those who found themselves newly splattered upon.

These attacks, at first seemingly random, became more sinisterly purposeful, as the confusion of the bloodbath afforded an opportunity for past slights and old scores to be settled. The furor usually continued until the farmer came out and ended it, but occasionally, subdued by sheer exhaustion, the flock would cease hostilities out of a sense of mutual self-preservation thinly disguised as a modicum of decorum.

The air was now filling with the sound of clucking tongues that, rising in a shrill cacophony of accusation, heralded the impending execution of the mother and her chick.

That is until a familiar figure interrupted the proceedings. Acting as though he were absentmindedly pausing in the middle of an afternoon stroll, Bantam, without offering even the slightest suggestion or gesture of defiance, and seemingly oblivious to the situation, quietly inserted himself squarely between the closing aggressor and his prey.

Frustrated and inwardly enraged, the would-be attacker held his ground for a few long seconds as he waited for the rooster to move while the flock, intrigued to see the outcome of the impasse, quieted down. Bantam, with seeming indifference, held his ground, affording his potential antagonist the opportunity to count the cost before going into battle. The Ruester, thinking better of open confrontation, and as casually as possible, chose to mimic Bantam's air of nonchalance. Passing by his intended victims as if they did not exist, the would-be attacker sauntered off as though he too had merely taken a reflective pause in the midst of an afternoon stroll.

Quickly dissembling in an effort to distance themselves from any identification with the embarrassment felt by the retreating and infuriated Ruester one by one the flock silently followed suit. Meanwhile the mother and her chick slipped quietly and gratefully away, careful to refrain from being seen to openly acknowledge Bantam's 'careless' intervention.

In awe of his dad, the motionless and conflicted young eagle expelled a heavy sigh that betrayed the distress of what he felt was his own cowardice. Unable to look up into his father's eyes he heard Bantam in a soft voice, laden with mock fear, say, "Poop sticks to feathers son. Let's go home, . . . before I soil myself."

As they walked away together the old bird interceded further, "Don't be too hard on yourself kid. I had a reputation and experience to draw on and you didn't. Besides, that was a close call. If that situation had been allowed to go on for a few seconds longer the flock would have worked itself into a frenzy that I wouldn't have gotten myself into the middle of either. Truth be told, there have been times that I have stood by and watched and, more often than I would care to admit, I couldn't tell if it was more out of fear or wisdom that I did. Son, you'll learn that in the moment we all do what we have to do."

CHAPTER FOUR: THE VISITATION

The honesty of Norm's naïve questions had a way of probing deeply but this one triggered in Bantam, the master of brevity, an unusually long response—but then, some answers demand a full explanation:

"Have I ever been really scared, kid? Well, I've been scared lots of times but *really scared?* Funny you should ask because there was one particular time when I was and it happened in my very last public fight. Although I'd been in the ring over fifty times and I'd never been beaten, this time I was rusty, I hadn't fought in over a year; in fact, I was pretty much dragged out of retirement to face a bigger, faster, and meaner opponent.

"In all my travels he was one character that I definitely knew I never wanted to mix with. Even when he was younger and inexperienced I saw him easily take out guys who had similar fighting styles to mine. Back then they called me The Whirlwind 'cuz I'd figure out the other guy's stronger side and I'd retreat from it staying just out of reach, occasionally attacking his weak side, until tired from all the chasing and spinning he'd get confused, tired, or careless, and I'd suddenly turn and jump up and right back at him, going straight for his eyes. Most times, if we weren't hooded, the fight was over there and then, but even if we were hooded they would recoil instinctively, and there they'd be—stiff, still, upright, and wide open—and I'd just pick my spot, hit it hard, and keep hammering.

"This guy, though, never used his speed to chase anybody. He was not only willing to absorb punishment he almost seemed to enjoy it. He just kept coming on, deflecting blows and cutting down the angles until his opponent wore himself out. When he did make his moves they were lightning fast and deadly accurate. Technically he was beautiful to watch, he hardly reacted to anything, he simply went about his business, which was killing, and he did it with pleasure, which was something that I never learned to do."

"I guess anybody would have been scared of a mean bird like him, huh?" volunteered Norm.

"Yeah, anybody with any sense that is, but that wasn't what really scared me, 'cuz I went into that fight ready to die. My life up until then had been nothing but a lonely struggle for survival. This was before I had even met Ma Bantam, all I knew about life was kill or be killed and, live or die, I knew it would be my last time in the ring. The match had only been arranged because the farmer needed the purse that was being offered, win or lose, to save the farm; all he had to do was put me in the ring against that killer. He didn't want to do it, but I guess he must have been real desperate because it sure tore him up to put me in that fight."

"But Pa, what could be scarier than dying? Were you scared of being blinded, or crippled, or something?" asked the young eagle.

"Heck, yeah! That too! But, no, what really scared me was how the fight ended. It changed everything. It, it . . . it changed me!" Bantam, finding himself spluttering, paused before continuing.

"Like I described, he fought the way he usually did, and I had no choice but to fight the way I usually did; it was all I knew. I kept circling backward, buying time, and I gave him all my best moves, but he wasn't about to be fooled. Every now and again he'd nearly box me in, and I'd barely get out of his way, but not without getting hit hard. Once he got his beak into me so bad that I thought he'd taken my wing off! He'd seen me fight too and he didn't miss a trick. He was real ring-smart, which was what made him so dangerous. From the moment the fight began he methodically set about tearing me apart, and even though I managed to nick him good a couple of times, that just made him meaner, icier, and more remorseless—and then *HE* faked *ME*!

"He backed off, giving me the first bit of breathing room I'd had in the whole fight, which drew me very subtly toward the center of the ring, and then he leapt and lunged with both feet going straight for my eyes—and we weren't hooded. I reared back hard and fast, and while I was still in midair, helplessly waiting for my feet to touch down, I saw, too late, that he had pulled back and planted himself. He was all coiled up and ready to drive his beak into any part of me that he wanted."

Norm, transfixed by the story, for once in his life, was out of questions. Bantam, on the other hand, was in full flow. "He had me. It was like that slow-motion thing that sometimes happens when a disaster strikes. All I could do was twist in the air and try to deflect his blow and hope to roll out of reach when I hit the ground. But this was one smart bird, he didn't strike! He was way ahead of me. He just waited and pounced at the very moment I landed, but instead of going in for the kill with his beak he launched again with both of his feet at my throat. I half-turned in a futile attempt to dodge him, which meant that when his claws grasped me I was off-balance. I ended up underneath him, pinned by my neck to the ground.

"I was more than physically overpowered, I was in total shock! The fight had never been close. He had not only outclassed me he had totally humiliated me. I was completely overwhelmed. I was fresh out of ideas, and with his whole weight on my throat I was running out of air, and I'd never ever seen anyone successfully fight from off the dirt, especially against the likes of him. I knew I was a goner for sure, and then *IT* happened. He froze!"

Bantam might have paused for effect or it might have been that he needed to collect himself from the awful memory of the event. In a slow, almost reverential, tone he continued, "But when I say he froze, I should say he was frozen. For just a moment his eyes kind of went vacant and his grip loosened. It was like suddenly he wasn't all there!

"I'd seen a look similar to the one he had on his face before, but only on birds that were fixin' to die, and this guy was far from that. It's not like he gave up, or that he spaced out, and it sure wasn't 'cuz he was in a merciful mood! For just a moment it was like something intervened, he was just taken out, he wasn't . . . ," and here the old rooster's voice ascended a couple of octaves as he sputtered, "he wasn't in control!

"I mean," the rooster tried to explain, "for just a moment it was like he lost it, or rather, *IT* lost him, and the moment didn't last long. Just before he started to come out of it I reacted and then so did he . . . but too late! His grip on me had loosened and in sheer desperation I pushed up against his gut with both my feet and levered him off the ground, and as he fell, quite literally the last thing he saw through his left eye was my beak."

"D-di-did you kill him, Dad?"

"I'm not sure. I was so scared though that I didn't dare stop attacking him. I gave him everything I had. Even half-blind he would have been dangerous, maybe more so, so I kept going at his head and neck until they plucked me out of there. I don't know what happened to him after the fight but, even if he lived, he wasn't ever going to return to the ring.

"I was so beat up that on the way home the farmer didn't put me in the box in the back of the truck like he usually did. Instead, he propped me up on a couple of cushions in the cab on the seat right next to him. And then he said, 'What happened out there, old fella? He had you dead to rights. I figured that there was no way that you could have simply muscled your way out from under that killer. I know it, you know it, and that bird sure knew it. Somebody up there must have had a reason for letting you live, and all I can say is, whatever that reason is, I'm sure mighty glad!'

" 'What I do know is that your fighting days are over, for good this time, and no more living alone in the barn for you. You saved the farm, the least I can do is let you enjoy the company of your own kind and, heck, yeah, I'd been thinking to do it anyway, maybe we'll see if we can't find you a little lady to call your own.'

"I must have slept for an entire week after that fight, and it took a lot longer than that for me to mend up, but he was true to his word. One day he came to the barn with his wife and kids, and first off, they made a great to-do over setting on fire a real fancy-looking piece of paper, and then he picked me up and carried me out of there and, at one and the same time, gave me both the worst and the best gifts of my life. The worst gift was putting me in this here roost, because I'd come to enjoy the peace of that barn—yet this coop must be the craziest place in the world!

"On the other hand, that was when I got introduced to Ma. And the time we had together, even though she's gone now, more than makes up for every day that I have lived, or ever will live in this place."

CHAPTER FIVE: FLYING ON THE GROUND

When a young eagle that does not know that he is an eagle finds himself growing up in a chicken coop, he has some serious questions. Questions that come from so deep they do not quite get fully framed in the head but the heart will persist in asking.

Although Bantam had a lot of answers, and although he knew a lot about life, he knew enough to know that there was plenty he knew nothing about. One thing he knew that he knew nothing about was about being an E. Gull. So, on those nights when his son stole out of the roost he learned to keep his eyes shut tight. More than once he had to stifle a snorted chuckle as the large young bird tripped and stumbled in his clumsy attempts to silently negotiate through the darkened confines of the roost and escape into the open secret of the night.

On one of Norm's earlier sorties, a minute or so after his son's exit, Bantam did follow his son at a very discreet distance. As he approached the western perimeter of the coop he beheld, outlined in the luminescence of a full lunar orb, the breathtaking silhouette of Norm with his majestic wings completely outstretched.

Bantam knew holy ground when he was standing on it, and that something in his son was crying from deep to deep, and that the intimacy of those depths are unspeakable, and very, very private. So, very quietly he respectfully retreated to his roost, and never again followed Norm on his nocturnal sojourns, and he never, never enquired about them.

When they did occur, Norm always headed toward the same spot at the western extremity of the coop. In the light of day Norm had observed the silhouette of a distant mountain range lazily punctuated by tiny moving dots that continually spiraled in hypnotic dances above it. This sight, and his nighttime remembrances of it, always elicited a tug in his heart which was known only to him, not only because only an eagle could know it but also because only an eagle could see it!

Ever inquisitive, earlier in his young life he had enquired of Bantam and Ma, and some of the chickens, if they felt the same way about what they saw out there. From their confused, incredulous, and sometimes derisive replies it became evident to him that chickens cannot see very far at all. They were not only totally unaware of the almost perpetually orbiting specks in the distance—they were not even aware of the mountains!

In the anonymity of the night Norm would point himself into the cool evening breeze and staring out into the star-studded darkness he would unfurl and stretch out his great wings. Hour after hour he bathed in the currents and gusts of air that gently flowed and sometimes playfully tumbled and pulled as they caressed and teased him. What he was enjoying went far beyond his comprehension because it was more than the soothing massage of wind passing over and through feathers that was stirring him, it was the exquisite overture of an unknown purpose and undreamt destiny—it was the promise of life itself!

At times the sensation became so strong that the spirit of the young eagle would soar ecstatically and only the unconscious restraint of years of incarceration prevented him from releasing an exultant screech that would surely have woken the entire coop. On these occasions he also became cognizant of the acutely stinging effect of the streaming night air and how easily it made his eyes fill with tears, but he barely dwelt on the superfluity of the irritation, as his heart, exulting in an unidentified emotion, swelled up and threatened to burst within his chest. Without an ounce of recognition about what he was feeling, or of what was happening to him, the young eagle wept silently and unashamedly in solitude, utterly abandoned to the sheer beauty of release.

CHAPTER SIX: FED UP

Tuesdays and Fridays were the young eagle's favorite mornings of the week because the farmer's wife would search him out and very specifically deposit a special pile of feed just for him. That is, they used to be his favorite days until one Tuesday, in mid-mouthful, he caught Bantam quirkily shaking his head.

"What is it, Pa?" he asked.

"Oh, nothing." replied Bantam evasively and just a little too hastily.

The puzzled and faintly disappointed look on Norm's face convinced the rooster that if he was to retain the trust that he had so carefully nurtured in the young bird he would have to deal with the question forthrightly.

"Okay," he added quickly, "I guess there's something I need to tell you. But I sure would hate to put you off your food."

"It would take a lot to do that, Dad," laughed Norm confidently, and he was right because during the two years of his young life his stomach had learned to digest what was far from an ideal diet for an eagle.

Bantam pointed across the farmyard and remarked, "Remember kid, I used to live in that barn, and in that place I saw and learned a lot of things that a chicken isn't supposed to see or know. One day you might need to learn a lot more about some of the things that went on over there,[1] but for today let's just talk about what happens to Friars on their journey from the coop to the barn, and . . ." he added slowly and ominously, "their journey back out of there. Did you ever wonder why or where they were going, or what happened to them when they got there?"

---

[1] Bantam's earlier experiences can be found in "The Barn Chronicles: The Collected Wisdom of a Professional Cockfighter."

"Well, a little bit, but I figured as I wasn't a Friar it wasn't my business to know," replied the youngster.

"No, you are not a Friar," affirmed Bantam with relief, "but the first couple of times I saw the farmer's wife give you your 'E. Gull's supplement,' as she calls it, I was worried that you just might be one of them. However, when she first began feeding you, you were only a chick, and what you were being fed was definitely not your normal chicken feed! I've always believed it must be something that a bird like you might ordinarily eat," gulped Bantam uneasily, "because you have certainly always seemed to enjoy it!"

The youngster failed to catch the hesitation caused by the choked-down revulsion in his father's voice, as he happily polished off the Tuesday special.

Waiting patiently for Norm to finish brunch, the old bird considered his next words carefully. "All right, son. Let's get down to basics. What is the death rate of chickens?"

After a slight pause Norm answered, "Well, I don't know. It's not something I have really thought about. Besides, it depends what you mean by . . ."

Bantam interrupted with an abrupt finality, "One hundred percent! The death rate of chickens is one hundred percent. Death comes to every chicken, it's a never-changing constant." And, with the serious subject of chicken mortality having now been addressed, Bantam pressed on with another question. "But you'll rarely, if ever, see a Friar die in this coop. So where do you think they do die?"

While the eagle pondered his question, Bantam, with slow and deliberate drama, raised a wing and pointed it toward the barn. Norm, knowing that his dad never made an empty gesture, carefully followed the direction of the overly theatrical movement.

Bantam steadfastly maintained his pose while he watched the innocent puzzlement on Norm's face slowly give way to a look of disbelief that, in turn, was eclipsed by the foreboding realization of a dark truth. Satisfied that the awful fact was now being contemplated, Bantam said emphatically, "Yep! That is where Friars go to die. And that's only the first stop on their journey! The farmer takes them into the barn and with one quick twist of their necks they are gone, and that, by the way, is why only on Saturdays, or the Sabbath, as the Friars like to call it, he is careful to close the door to the barn behind him. It also explains why just a few minutes after the farmer enters the barn with a live chicken you see him carrying something out to the farmhouse in a sack—and why he also returns to the barn a few minutes later with that same sack empty!"

Norm, recollecting the frequency and the pattern of the farmer's Saturday routine, aided by the gravity in Bantam's voice, was quick to accede to the conclusion that the evidence pointed to.

"But why?" he asked incredulously. "What's the point in feeding-up a bird and then killing it? And why take it to the farmhouse?"

Bantam could see that Norm was on the verge of being unable to think clearly, and he was too kind to leave his son to grope agonizingly slowly toward a conclusion that might have proven too repugnant to be entertained by a youngster with such tender sensibilities.

With well-developed timing and the fearlessness of one who never flinched from the truth he bluntly remarked, "More to eat, boy. More to eat."

"What!" exclaimed the outraged eagle. "The Friars are eaten! Who by? By the humans?! That can't be, th-th-that . . . just can't be!"

"But it is," declared Bantam, "and that is why they are taken for that trip in the sack. 'Cuz humans eat chickens, and what's really weird is that after stripping them they like to burn them up some. At some of my outdoor fights I've even seen them invite their friends over to do it at what they call *barbecues*."

Norm, with his heart pounding and his head spinning, slumped to the ground while Bantam waited for an opening. The worst was yet to come and he knew there would probably not be a better time to deliver it.

And sure enough the youngster provided the opening. "Why are you telling me all this?" asked the eagle with the guarded hesitation of the compulsive enquirer who has already heard enough unpleasant truth for one day.

"Because you asked me, son."

"When, Dad?"

"When you saw me shaking my head. I didn't mean for you to see me do that, but you did. And what you saw me shaking my head at was your enjoyment of your 'special' meal."

Bantam did not wait for any further questions as at length he proceeded to describe the process of how, in the barn, he had witnessed the carcass and guts, feathers and feet, claws and beaks of a chicken, cooked or not, being ground up into meal for consumption by animals and birds.

The clinical dissertation on the final disposal of the remains of Friars and the pointed emphasis that Bantam had put on the feeding of "meal" to "birds" gave the quick and clever young eagle just enough time and information to gather himself to make the terrible synaptic leap.

"You can't mean that I've been eating . . . ?" deduced the youngster as his voice trailed off into the unspeakable, fractured mumblings of disgust.

"I'm afraid so, son," Bantam softly concluded, and added, "I sampled some of your earlier feeds and in my fights I've sunk my beak into enough birds to know that without doubt most of that stuff they have been feeding you, well . . . " And now even the battle-hardened old veteran had to steel himself, "Well, . . . it tastes like chicken!"

Turning hastily the youngster lost his breakfast.

Over the following weeks the farmer's wife noticed that Norm had suddenly gone off his feed. Her husband concluded incorrectly that the young eagle had outgrown his diet but stumbled upon the perfect solution by beginning to hand-feed the young eagle scraps of raw meat. These feedings did more than improve Norm's condition and fill out his frame and size; they also fed some wild misconceptions in the coop.

Fearful whispered guesses about Norm's special diet and his relish in it provoked gossip that, unchecked, quickly became established in the annals of coop lore. Much to Bantam's amusement he eventually discovered that the flock had come to believe that the gentle-hearted Norm was being groomed by his much-storied father and the farmer to become the ultimate fighting machine. The largeness of the young eagle and his wickedly long talons, and his large, viciously curved beak helped maintain the easily frightened chickens in their fiction. At bedtime, mothers subdued unruly chicks by issuing dire and forbidding warnings that any continued misbehavior might well invite a late-night visitation from the formidable bird.

In the absence of truth perception becomes reality, and in the dangerous hazard of coop life Bantam appreciated that the myth afforded his son a certain degree of protection. In the complicity of silence he played along with the myth, but lies, even useful ones, have a way of causing complications.

CHAPTER SEVEN:
TOO LITTLE, TOO LATE—ALMOST

"Dad, Dad, guess what! You'll never guess what happened!"

In an effort to temper his son's outburst Bantam answered casually, "Let me see now, did the farmer double up on your daily feed? No, no," he jokingly mused, "or did that rip in his pants finally blow wide open? Uhhmmm, no, it's got to be something much more important, could it be that we are going to be getting those new electrified henhouses that I've been hearing about?"

"Aw, Pa, stop kidding around, this is something serious. I mean, I could never have guessed that they would ask me."

"Who are 'they,' and what did they ask?" enquired the rooster with some concern.

Barely able to contain himself, the young eagle continued enthusiastically " 'They' are the Ruesters, and what they asked was, that after careful deliberation 'we,' meaning they, have decided to extend to 'you,' meaning me, a seat on the council. Dad, isn't it great?!"

In his excitement the young eagle was oblivious to Bantam's sigh. The old bird was well aware of how the roost was run. He knew that the Ruesters could not subdue Norm, and with the youngster's new reputation and Bantam's ever-watchful eye they were almost certainly too scared to attempt to kill him, so it was not surprising that they would make an attempt to win him over.

There was caution in the old rooster's words as he replied, "Well, it's certainly an honor, I guess, but . . . ," and then Bantam's voice trailed off as he began to reconsider. This was something that he probably could not talk the kid out of and maybe it was best that he should not even try.

"Perhaps", he thought grudgingly, "this is what the youngster needs"

"Sounds like a big decision. What does it involve? I mean, what do you have to do?" he asked with some misgivings.

"First off, on Friday evening I have to attend an extraordinary meeting where they officially extend to me my invitation to become 'an Honorable Fellow and Member in Good Standing of the Fraternal Order of the Most Noble Brotherhood and Lodge of the Royal Roost of Ruesters.' Dad, I'm going to be a member of the 'R.R.R.' We are in!"

Alarmed and disappointed at the ease and enthusiasm with which his son was succumbing to the tentacles of seduction Bantam retorted, "*We* are, are *we*?" and noticing that this did not provoke even the faintest flicker of a response in the eyes of the inductee-to-be, he fired another salvo of sarcasm in a forlorn attempt to wrest his boy from the ever-tightening coils of indoctrination, "and what else do *we* have to do to get in?"

Alerted by the edge in Bantam's voice the young bird defensively replied, "Well, I have only just joined. I mean I haven't joined quite yet, but even you have said that there has to be a purpose to my being here in this coop, and maybe this is it," but being checked by the hurt in his father's eyes, he quickly added, " . . . or part of it, anyways."

Bantam now knew that further criticism would be futile, even counterproductive, so he concluded their conversation as quietly and cheerfully as he could. Over the coming days Bantam made a determined attempt to share in as much of the youngster's excitement as he could, but for the first time in their lives an uncomfortable silence had come between them. Bantam really missed his wife not being there to gently remind him to be patient because now there was nothing left to do but wait, and in that time of lonely waiting he took a fearless inventory of his own soul.

And he came to a stunning realization. An awful truth flooded him, and with typical courage he faced it. He had failed. It was not that he did not love his son, he did, but he simply had to acknowledge his blindness or stubbornness, or both. Without ascribing blame to others he sadly accepted that he did not know very much about what it was to be a father. The little he knew about his own parents was gleaned from brief, distant, and hazy memory and, coupled with the lonely life he had led as a fighting cock, it had left him poorly equipped to be anyone's dad, let alone a bird like Norm, who, suddenly, had come, or was coming, of age.

Bantam had become accustomed to loneliness. It had become a comfort and a refuge to him, but it was now a luxury his son could no longer afford. The boy, wherever he had come from, had been raised in the coop, and as much as Bantam detested that thought, it was his home, and if he was to live here Norm needed to know its history. Sure, the boy had a working knowledge of the dynamics and dangers of coop life, but there was so much that Bantam had not cared to learn and so could not share. It had now become evident that the youngster needed to be exposed to other well-versed and learned opinions— commodities in rare supply in the coop.

However, there was Magnus, a bird universally accepted as being possessed of uncommon knowledge, experience, and wisdom. So Bantam arranged for and then invited Norm to accompany him on an afternoon visit to Magnus's roost, a simple but very clean and well-maintained abode. Many chickens were drawn there by the sense of welcome and well-being Magnus exuded, but only a few would dare gather around him as he reminisced about happier and more prosperous days when he had been a more prominent member of the coop.

As a rule the chickens were careful not to be seen to be too close to Magnus, or to be too enamored of him, as he was considered by the ever-vigilant Süds to be a dangerous figure. However, because the Ruesters' dominance relied, at least in part, upon the honoring of tradition they were careful to speak well of him in public, but even then their compliments were muted by the damnation of faint praise. The Süds, however, were more than willing to condemn Magnus's followers as being simple, outdated, and incapable of, if not impediments to, progress.

Norm greeted Magnus in the usual wry manner that his band and a small minority of the coop reserved for each other. Whoever spoke first would say, "The roosts . . . " and the other would reply, "are the roots," and Bantam's offering of the opening greeting was met with its customary response by Magnus and the other chickens. All of them lived their lives in the same quiet, forthright, and careful manner as Magnus, and they all shared in and enjoyed his same resolute but kind and cheerful demeanor, and all of them delighted in his down-to-earth humorous quips that so warmly penetrated and sustained their souls.

The usual and genuine pleasantries were exchanged and an easy conversation began, but Norm, preoccupied by his upcoming R.R.R. membership was not his usual attentive self, although he politely stood alongside Bantam while his father prodded Magnus toward reflection.

"The early days," Bantam asked, "what made them so different from today?"

"Well, there's a lot to be said on that," replied Magnus, "but, if you want to get to the heart of the matter, it's this. Every roost had its own rooster. That is, it was run in the way he wanted it to be run. He decided on everything that went on in his roost, he was responsible for every chicken in his roost, and, if a chicken didn't like the way the roost was run, they were always free to search for a roost more to their liking—or sleep outside and forage for themselves. Nobody was forced to live in a particular roost because they could always vote with their feet."

"Some roosts were better than others, some were stricter, some were more easygoing, some were clean, and some were not so clean. But whatever the head-rooster of the roost said in his roost was law. You see, back then there was a basic understanding that all chickens, even the most noble ones among us, were not only capable of doing extremely good but also extremely bad things, so no one chicken, or group of chickens, was ever meant to be entrusted with total power and control over the entire coop. So, back in the days when the chickens lived in the original thirteen houses that are now on the eastern perimeter of the coop all chickens were free to pursue their lives wherever they wished. However, during the time of the great expansion when the co-op really grew, other chicken breeds were constantly being introduced, and most of them were very different, but, for the most part, they were hardy, adaptable, productive, and contributed to the co-op, but there was one breed that slipped in which had a completely different notion on the nature of chickens and the ruling of roosts."

Here Bantam chimed in. "That would be The Pseuds?"

"Yes, it would. The Bearded Strutters. The first ones came from a town called Frankfurt in the south of a country called Germany, and then others who thought just like them followed from nearby towns. In their native language *Süd*, S-Ü-D, means 'South' so they kind of clubbed together under that name."

"Why, that's a new one on me," remarked Bantam. "I always wondered why such a self-important and humorless bunch could tolerate being identified as phonies, by being called Pseuds, P-S-E-U-D-S."

"Yep, language, and how we hear it, is a funny thing, and those guys sure know how to use it. They're never happier than when they're using big fancy 'You're-a-peon' words.

Knowing that he was shortly destined for instruction by and in the ways of The Süds, Norm was quickened to enter the conversation. "What exactly does 'You're-a-peon' mean?"

"A good question, and I'm not too sure of the answer but, judging from their air of superiority, and their way of looking down their beaks, it might just mean what it says, that they think everyone else is a peon, and that nobody else quite measures up to their elevated standards." As Magnus said this, he awkwardly mimicked the beak-in-the-air, and stiff, jerky perambulation and neck movements of the Süds.

Everybody chuckled except for Bantam, who fell about in hysterics which seemed a little overdone as Magnus's theatrics weren't that well executed or that original, but finally managing to steady himself Bantam explained, "Why, I thought it meant this . . . !" as he turned his back on the group and cocked his leg up as though he were about to relieve himself.

Now everybody fell about laughing. "Well, that fits too, I guess," agreed Magnus with a chortle, "and all those explanations fit the bill, but those birds take themselves and what they believe in very seriously, which is why, although both they and the Friars support the Ruesters, they and the Friars can never get along."

Magnus cleared his throat and began to explain further. "The Friars, of course, believe in a Creator and a better life beyond this one. This runs absolutely contrary to the Süds who are forever trying to convince those who believe in them to trust in them and believe that, after a few unfortunate and necessary inconveniences, we can turn this coop into a paradise for all."

"If we would just knuckle under their collective wisdom (even though they can't agree among themselves), they promise to spare us the rigors and privations of individual effort and failure. Instead they promote 'a fair and collective equality for all,' excluding themselves of course. According to them we would all become one happy society if each roost came under their careful and watchful guidance. When I retired from office I warned that the enforced dictates of these 'Commissars of compassion' would be cold and cruel substitutes for kind and willing hearts full of charity.

"The Süds support Garic, and those like him, because he is acclimating the coop to an authoritarianism that will ultimately be displaced by a much more thorough authoritarianism—their own. Which brings me full circle. They assiduously, tirelessly, and deliberately undermine and seek to destroy the importance and value of individual choice and freedom and any roosts that nurture such notions. They won't be happy until everyone comes under the authority of the Central Henhouse. If they ever succeed it'll be the end of whatever freedoms we have left."

"So, you don't believe in being organized or governed?" asked Norm.

"Oh, yes I do, young fella. All of us have weaknesses and problems, so we need laws, to which we should all be equally subject, that help us to cooperate with, and to guard ourselves from hurting, each other. What I fear is not government. I want every rooster to govern his own roost. No, what I fear is a centralized elite that commands and organizes how everyone should think and behave—or else."

"You see, in the early days each rooster used to meet with the other roosters about once a week. They represented their respective roosts and the interests of those in their care, and they agreed on some very basic rules, known as The Foundations, that would help the general welfare of the whole co-op, but little by little they spent more and more time with the other roosters and less and less time in their roosts. That brought about less relationship and more rules, and less relationship and more rules, and less relationship and more rules, and so The Foundations were gradually eroded."

"Well, can't the rules that go against The Foundations be reversed? Or what if The Foundations just don't work anymore?" asked Norm.

"This is one bright kid," observed Magnus to Bantam. "That's why we have The Mendings. If seventy-five percent of the roosts agree, which is not as easy to do as it might sound, The Foundations can lawfully be altered. However," and now Magnus's voice dropped to a dark whisper, "there is another way of changing things. The co-op relied on what was then the Seven Supreme Elders, who, thanks to Garic's grandfather, are now the Nine Supreme Elders, birds that have The Foundations memorized, who are charged with passing on the legacy of The Foundations to each new generation. But the Süds apparently never understood the concept of freedom, either because they came from a place where freedom had never been enjoyed like it was in the days of the co-op, or they were simply just so full of themselves that when they got here they never recognized or valued it. Their arrogance can be directly attributed to their ignorance; the question is, is their ignorance genuine or is it a convenient cloak for their 'good' intentions?

"Either way, they used the trickery of their words to replace The Foundations! It has taken time but the coop has pretty much fallen under their spell. They have now usurped the authority of the roosts with the Grand Congress, mostly through the replacing of The Foundations with their pseudo-facts and pseudo-welfare. In the vacuum left by the relationships that had been nurtured in the roosts, many of the young have been led away from their families and brainwashed by the collective wisdom of the Süds. The more desperate, naïve, and ambitious amongst them dutifully eat up everything that is put in front of them, hence our name for these little know-it-alls—Peckerheads.

"The tipping point came when the Süds gained control over the co-op food supply. A long time ago, when there were fewer henhouses each roost would be given its daily feed by the farmer, a roost that produced more eggs got more feed, and each rooster determined who got how much to eat. This meant that chickens were rewarded for their efforts, or they moved on to where they were more appreciated. Care was given to the young, elderly, and the sick, but not to those who were lazy.

"But then, during the days that the co-op grew so quickly, the farmer thought it would be more efficient if we all got our food from a central trough, which resulted in the free-feed, where so much fighting occurred and food got trampled on and wasted, that many weak and sick, and young and old birds got hardly anything, or nothing, to eat.

"The Süds, always quick to seize on a crisis, suggested the institution of a new order of who got to eat, how much, and when—the Fare Deal. The Ruesters, being too few in number and much too important to be troubled by such mundane matters, were happy to accept the Süds's suggestion and commissioned them to devise and implement their plan. This plan is complicated by lots of Exceptions, so it takes a lot of management, especially as it is constantly being adjusted by the Süds. So, in exchange for food bonuses and priority in nest building and selection, more and more chickens became enrolled as Agents and Organizers, whose function is to help the Süds oversee and enforce the doling out of the food, according, of course, to what their determination of the needs of the flock are.

"As always, the Ruesters got to eat first, and to eat as much as they liked, then the Friars were next and, although they are only a tiny portion of the flock, sacred tradition meant that they got their Divine Ten Percent. Then each of the Süds, being the implementers of the plan, made sure they got their share. Whatever is left is doled out to the lay-chickens by the Süds and their Agents, but because the numbers of the Süds, their appointees, and their appetites keep growing, there is increasingly less food left over after they have eaten.

"You may have noticed that those who have continued to live under the cover of their own roosts, and who tend to the needs of those that they love and live amongst, are awarded smaller portions so they have to forage harder, deeper, and smarter to find scraps, bugs, and worms in order to survive. However, those that enforce the will of the Ruesters and the Süds, and their Agents, along with the silent and benign complicity of the Friars, get fatter and greater in numbers. This elite has subverted The Foundations and have ensconced themselves as the rulers and arbiters of the Süd System. They never abide by the same 'enlightened' rules that are put upon the lay-chickens, nor do they ever deign to actually live among them, and should they ever experience lack or hunger early in their careers, it's not for long and they never let anyone ever forget about it."

These last words were almost spat out by Magnus, who was careful to punctuate his oft-repeated extemporaneous lecture with an almost rhetorical question. "And we know the name that these champions of the coop and their supporters operate under, don't we . . . ?"

The almost rhetorical question was met with a universal and contemptuous response by those gathered around Magnus as they breathed out the answer in a small chorus of defiance, "The Fed!"

Later that day, back at his roost Bantam reflected that although Norm had listened to Magnus, and even asked a couple of pertinent questions during their visit, he was not his normally highly engaged and inquisitive self—and over the next couple of days following the visit the expected torrent of questions that were usually forthcoming from the thoughtful young bird were not asked. It seemed that most of the information had fallen on deaf ears.

Norm remained more silent than usual, and over the coming days the silence grew, and Bantam became increasingly aware that for the first time a painful gulf of separation had grown between them.

CHAPTER EIGHT: THE ZEALOT

Norm, oblivious of the void that Bantam felt and with all the enthusiasm of a recent convert busied himself with the demands of his new membership. Beginning early, he would position himself to intercept Garic and courteously greet the Most High Ruester as he descended from the roof of the main henhouse after his daily discharging of the farm alarm. He also attended and listened dutifully to the morning klatch, an informal but prestigious gathering of the aspiring-to-be-most-senior Ruesters.

Here matters of both subtle and great importance were discussed. The young eagle never spoke during these meetings but he learned to appreciate the vital importance of coop discipline and how assiduous and unfailingly alert the Ruesters, aided by the Süds, were in detecting even the slightest of infractions that might militate against the order of the flock.

At first, some of the observations and judgments of the klatch seemed too severe and discomfiting, but he quickly learned to suppress his concerns. Especially when it was repeatedly stated that, of course, nobody enjoyed having to attend to such business, but that some things, no matter how small or unpleasant, simply had to be dealt with for the greater good.

The young bird also realized that he was obviously destined to not only make strides, but to blaze a trail 'on the path of enlightenment' as he was learning to call it. Recognition amongst those who had now become his peers, and the increased attention and even deference that was being extended to him, even by some of the elder Ruesters, was most gratifying to Norm as he grew in knowledge and in the powers of persuasion, which were somewhat aided, and not always unconsciously, by the sheer enormity of his physical presence. Eventually he learned to no longer be embarrassed by his size but to parade it for the benefit and admiration of all.

Norm's daily schedule also meant that his nocturnal meditations became less frequent, and also less reflective, as in his increasingly diminishing private moments he dedicated himself to the higher level of personal grooming demanded by his newfound position. He especially paid attention to the disfiguring thin streak of white feathers that ran through the inside of his left wing, which, without regular plucking, marred his otherwise flawlessly majestic plumage.

The daily instruction by the Süds was informative and exhaustive, but Magnus's colorful depiction of the more zealous and gullible students as Peckerheads, and his years of observing and acquiring Bantam's disdain for mindless repetition kept Norm from fully ingesting and regurgitating the proud rhetoric of their Squawking Points as unquestionable truth.

With the sole exception of Garic, Xen and the Rev. Deed stood atop the Ruester hierarchy, and it was Garic who had privately charged the distinguished pair with the oversight of Norm's preparation for his future role on the Council. The young eagle came to appreciate that Xen was a most cerebral and wise bird, and that the noble and upright Reverend, underneath his crusty exterior, had a kindly and solicitous heart. That such profoundly venerated souls dedicated so much time to him was at first flattering, but then, thanks to his newly enlightened state, Norm understood that he needed to transcend this self-consciousness and accept with humility that the attention being lavished upon him was predicated by the burden of his now much-lauded giftedness nature and calling. This realization also helped Norm to make the uncomfortable break from Bantam's roost when he was invited to the cramped but much-coveted upper reaches of the main loft where he slept between the ever-watchful Xen and the Rev. Deed.

Though neither one of these two luminaries could fully convince Norm of the veracity of their conflicting philosophies, he bathed in their attention as they vied for control of his mind and soul—and the future domination of the coop. He was at first drawn to the Rev. Deed's teaching that posited faith in an all-powerful Creator who supposedly radiated unconditional love, but Norm was disturbed by the Reverend's occasionally contradictory and dire warnings of the eternally severe and even capriciously cruel punishments of this Absolute Being.

On the other hand, Norm enjoyed the challenge of the rigorous disciplining demanded by Xen, although it clashed with the benign evasiveness of the whimsical Ascended Master, who had no answers as to the origin or conclusion of anything. The seemingly enlightened one pushed Norm's deeper philosophical questionings into the murky polysyllabic cosmic soup of an indeterminate past or a perennially deferred future. Also, Xen's habit of answering Norm's earnest questions with his own nonsensical questions, such as, "If a chicken lays a log in a forest, and no one is there to hear it, what is the sound of one hen crapping?" quickly wore thin.

The young eagle tried to embrace the expansiveness of Xen's 'eternal now' but thanks to his relationship with Ma and Bantam he had simply become too accustomed to the intercourse of affection to blindly accept that everything came out of an impersonal nothingness, or that the "is-ness" just "was" and always "was and would be". Besides, he thought, as he tirelessly distilled all of Xen's teachings, *what is "is," and what is the purpose of "is"*?

Nevertheless, after morning instruction he would occasionally be encouraged by Xen or the Rev. Deed to share some of his newfound insights in the presence of Garic. Life, indeed, was rich, full, and challenging but the disciplines of his daily duties as a novitiate and his exalted position in the roost had now made his nocturnal meditations utterly impossible. Besides, they were hardly missed, and neither was Bantam.

CHAPTER NINE: THE GRAND GALA

The night of the Grand Gala was the coop's social event of the year. Held in The Great Congress on midsummer night, the occasion was marked by the annual presentation of awards and the opportunity to parade newly acquired titles and promotions that had been handed out within the roost hierarchy. Custom dictated that the proceedings usually opened with the very dignified and solemn recalling of those names that had been added to the Friars' Hall of Fame. A family member or friend would lay the feather of a dearly departed one into the soft sand immediately below the Roosts of Privilege, sacred territory that was normally reserved for the passage of Ruesters and, grudgingly, the humans. This memorial service was known as the Nom de Plume, some said because of the commemorative feather itself, but others held that it was on account of the smoke that billowed thickly and darkly from the chimney on the farmer's house on Sunday mornings, a signal which had long become associated with the acceptance of a "chosen one".

This year, however, was to be different. Quite infrequently, perhaps only once or twice in the life of a chicken would they get to witness the formal admission of a new member to the Council. The festivities were to commence as they usually did with the pomp and ceremony of the Procession of the Grand Council, featuring the Ruesters who, from the least to the greatest in ascending order of seniority, paraded down the center aisle of the coop that was almost menacingly lined by the Süds. One by one they would occupy their places of office on their respective tiers of the Perches of Privilege. Firstly, the lower and much longer Bar of the Council was filled by its members and then immediately above it The Rung of Eldership was occupied by Xen and the Rev. Deed, and then finally Garic would install himself above them all on the Perch of Power. Once all the members of The Pyramid of the Grand Council had been ensconced this would normally have signaled that the ceremonies were to commence, starting with the Nom de Plume.

After the observation of the Nom de Plume, the award ceremonies proper would begin. Many honors were conferred upon the lay-chickens, but never any promotions, with two of the most earnestly coveted being the White Beak Award, given to the chicken that was considered the most polite and respectful, and the self-explanatory Biggest Egg of the Year Award.

The highest lay-award, the Hot Chick, however, was given to the hen that had supplied the most eggs in the previous year. This recognition accorded absolute nesting privileges, granting its recipient the right to select and change at will the nest of their preference throughout the coming year. All honors and awards were granted and recognized on the holy ground immediately below the Bar of the Council.

Amid much squawking and clucking, the awards ceremony was concluded by a ritual dance, known as the Diss-play. Although the dance was freestyle it was pretty much a compulsory exercise for the better-endowed lay-chickens who, on this one occasion in the year, were allowed to publicly turn their backs on the Ruesters. Facing the body of the coop, they would begin by first slowly dragging their tail feathers side-to-side in the dust, and then, gradually picking up the tempo of their movement and the attitude of their rumps, would finish with a wildly ecstatic flurry as they climaxed their gyrations with a full fanning of their tail feathers. If there was a time in the year when the coop lost all sense of propriety this was it—with even the normally stoic and aloof Ruesters showing some excitement!

This year, however, with the opening procession having been completed and with all other chickens and Ruesters in neat array, the festivities were to begin with Garic regally giving Norm the Nod of Approval. The newest member to the Council was then to march in solitary dignity down the center aisle, ascend the Ladder of the Wise, and then occupy his place at the end of the Bar of the Council.

Norm, although careful not to show it, could hardly wait for the gala, although his enthusiasm had been lessened by his father's gentle but firm declining of the front-row seat that his son had offered to him. Despite being hurt by Bantam's refusal, because Bantam never attended the Grand Gala, the young bird's love and respect for his father, aided of course by his newfound enlightenment, made him secretly vow that he would use his position of prestige to ensure the perpetual welfare of his dad. "After all", he magnanimously thought to himself, "it is the least I can do."

The big night finally came; the farmer and his wife had left in their truck as they did every year to attend the annual dance in town. The coop was in a partying mood! Norm's moment had almost arrived, everything had proceeded as it should, but, despite Norm's recent training in personal detachment, the young bird found himself suddenly and extremely nervous.

As Garic finally settled into position he signaled for Norm to conclude the stately procession. A hush fell upon the coop as the young eagle, with all eyes focused on him, lurched stiffly down the center aisle. One or two chickens, drunk in anticipation of the approaching reverie, attempted to stifle their giggles with muted coughs. These sounds only served to add to the unnerving of the acutely self-conscious youngster. By the time he had reached the bottom rung of the ladder below the Bar of the Council, he was aware of an unwelcome but unmistakable and uncontrollable loosening of his bowels.

Clenching as tightly as he could he awkwardly began his ascent, hoping that a telltale streak was not on full display before the attentive and up-turned faces of the flock below. Snickering turned into giggles, and giggles ballooned into guffaws as the young eagle, in a now obviously bespoiled condition, falteringly continued his erratic climb. The Ruesters, faces screwed tight with consternation at the seemingly irreverent and unwarranted behavior of the gathering below, suspiciously scrutinized the face of the ascending young bird, adding to Norm's panic.

Then came the final humiliation. Cramped by the confines of the gables which angled steeply upward into the apex of the roof, Norm, shaking nervously, tripped, which made him instinctively thrust out his wings to regain balance. Unfortunately the tip of his right wing collided with the underside of a beam, which catapulted him backward from the ladder. As he toppled, one foot flew out from under him while the other one succeeded in only gaining a momentary purchase on a rung. Mercifully his own fresh droppings kept him from maintaining his tenuous grip or he would have been left a dangling spectacle. Instead he crashed heavily into the soft sand below the Bar of the Council.

Now even the initially stunned Ruesters were obliged, in an effort to save face, to join the flock that had erupted in laughter at the plight of the hapless bird. Looking up into the front row of cackling beaks the only distinct voice he heard was that of the Rev. Deed's wife, who had never taken kindly to Norm's insistent and awkward questioning of her husband, as she shrilled "At least he can fall well!" To the young bird the scene was frighteningly reminiscent of one of the ritual sacrifices. Absolutely undone and in a state of blind panic he staggered to his feet and fled the roost, oblivious to the uproar he left behind.

Before he knew it he found himself outside his old home. Sobbing hard, and with his mind racing, he attempted to gather himself while he vainly searched for calm and comfort in the confused embarrassment of personal humiliation. Bantam, alerted by the distinctly heightened and unusually early sounds and commotion coming from the other side of the coop, had stolen occasional curious glances through the low door of his roost until he caught sight of a large and familiar shadow.

Peeking out, he was disturbed to see the trembling frame of his son. Having seen enough defeated and crushed animals in his life he recognized a broken spirit when he saw it, and he knew that whenever possible the badly hurt and wounded sought the safety and refuge of home. In due season the full story behind the events of the evening would follow, but for now whatever the circumstance, his boy was back.

Stepping outside, Bantam gently embraced his son and held him for a long, long time, straining to make sense of the fractured stream of words and apologies that were rendered almost unintelligible by the sobs which racked Norm's shaking body. Eventually, as the emotions ebbed and before the youngster could gather himself to try to speak again, the kindly rooster offered the first part of a couplet, "Son, as much as it might hurt right now you'll come to learn that there is one thing worse than being disillusioned," and after holding a lengthy pause he concluded, " . . . and that is being illusioned."

CHAPTER TEN:
STRAIGHT DOWN THE MIDDLE AND A LITTLE BIT HIGHER

The days immediately following the debacle of the Grand Gala were exquisitely painful for Norm. Under the merciless light of intense introspection his waking hours were filled with guilt, and at nights even the refuge of sleep was so haunted by shame that the young eagle found himself driven back to the familiar solace of his now more-than-somewhat-extended nocturnal meditations. Even though he had more time to himself he forsook the vanity of high-level grooming and almost welcomed the return of the scar of white feathers to his left wing as he began to learn to accept himself for whatever he was.

Initially his days were almost exclusively devoted to sleeping and napping in the cozy familiarity of Bantam's roost but little by little he began to venture out into the coop. Much to his relief it seemed that the chickens were trying to avoid him as much as he was trying to avoid them, and whenever there was any physical proximity it was attended by a studied silence and a careful lack of eye contact on both sides.

As time passed he weathered the largely self-perceived ridicule of the flock, and much later, in retrospect, he came to realize that the chickens hardly spent any time thinking about him and certainly not as much time as he spent thinking about himself. For the most part, Norm was spared too deep a descent into the pit of denial, as in installments he was able to recount his attempt to ascend the ranks of chickendom to his ever attentive and very understanding father.

Bantam's presence served as a constant reminder that he was loved, and that there was at least one kind opinion that contrasted and countered the coldness or indifference of the chickens. Clearly he had gifts and abilities, but they were not, evidently, to be placed at the feet of the coop, nor was it likely that they would ever again be welcomed by the flock.

With his foundation of belief and purpose having been so thoroughly shaken he began to think about eggs again—a lot. Lack of information meant that his own origin did not furnish him with much to ponder upon, so he found himself repeatedly musing on the question of the origin and purpose of everything and the philosophical mysteries that both preoccupied and divided Xen and the Rev. Deed.

As with the mystery concerning the origin of his own egg, where did the first egg come from? What did it come out of? What did it go into? What was it made from? What made it change? And where did the life in it and the ability for it to develop come from? Sometimes, even more darkly, he wondered was there a purpose for everything—or anything?

Finally, one evening, in his own inimitable way he inquired for answers from Bantam. The old bird chuckled before responding, "Son, as you know, we always figured that if you were old enough to ask a question, Ma and I always believed you were ready for the answer, and you are asking earnestly, which is important, because unless somebody is seriously wrestling with this particular question I've found that there is no point in answering it. But, I believe there is an answer, and I guess you're ready.

"Before we start, let me make clear, as much as I respect Magnus and agree with his insistence on honoring The Foundations, I am not convinced that they in themselves are the ultimate answer. You see, if the hearts of chickens were full of goodness it would make no difference what system of government we had. If you think about it, if that were the case, we actually wouldn't need to be governed. But we do need governing and, chickens being what chickens are, if we are ever going to move forward with any integrity we must either honor our foundations by following them, or change or remove them lawfully. Where I definitely agree with Magnus is that to say you are honoring The Foundations at the same time that you are going around them is to subvert established and agreed-upon law and replace it with the arbitrary rules of a dominant chicken or a ruling cadre. Our first order of business must be to recover The Foundations, or we shall simply be further crushed beneath the heel of those who control us through subtle deceit or the wielding of force—or both. And know this for sure, without Magnus and the other roosters who fight for the control of their own roosts, the Süds would have totally overrun the coop a long time ago.

"Furthermore, much to Magnus's credit, after presiding on the Perch of Power for two terms he refused a third term because he believed and taught that the real power had to belong to the chickens and that if the co-op needed anyone in office for three or more terms then it was doomed to failure. It was a gutsy move but Magnus put real talk in his squawk, and only time will tell whether the chickens live on as a co-op or a coop.

"Whatever the outcome, I am certain that the ultimate answer does not depend on how chickens wield power, although, for now, they have their part to play. Having said that, where do I begin?" mused Bantam.

"I believe that if someone shares a truth with you, they should be able to explain it simply, and they should leave you with the feeling that you were just let in on a secret that you kind of already knew. However, if you are left with the feeling that you are asking too many unwelcome or stupid questions then you are being stonewalled by someone who doesn't love you or who doesn't know or love the truth. If you are left feeling more confused, know this: you have been sold a bill of goods and you will find yourself being ensnared in mysteries."

"What's the difference between a secret and a mystery, Dad?" the young bird asked with a perception honed by his recent long hours of careful listening and debate with Xen and the Rev. Deed.

Bantam answered, "Well, a *secret* is something that you can understand but haven't yet been shown; but a *mystery* is something that can never be understood or unraveled. Be warned, character's that peddle in mysteries either do not have answers or they are hiding something."

"Xen and the Rev. Deed are hiding something?" asked the youngster.

"Maybe, but most probably they simply can't face the fact that they don't have an answer," replied Bantam. "I can say this much: Neither of them has the answer you are looking for. You see, they both labor under the same misconception; they persist in the vanity that somehow they are in control of their destiny. But the truth is Somebody else has a much bigger plan than theirs, an overwhelming plan which includes everything and everyone, including them, and that plan is taking all of us through the trials of this life and will bring us all home. Now that's a real beakful, so let me ask you a question. The Rev. Deed, you kind of got to like the idea of his God, but all his talk on eternal damnation was too hot to handle, right?"

"Why, yes Dad," responded the youngster, surprised at Bantam's grasp of the Rev. Deed's teachings.

"And, although you really liked Xen's acceptance of everything, he never gave you anything to hang on to except his exercises to purify yourself while you trudged along his interminable path of enlightenment?"

"Right again, Dad. Even though there were things I liked about what each of them said, they both fundamentally disagreed with each other and neither one of them could fully answer my questions."

"Son, you are right to say that they disagree with each other, but you are wrong when you say 'they fundamentally disagree,' because fundamentally they *agree*!" Surprised by Bantam's easy and swift plunge into philosophical discourse, Norm set himself to listen attentively to his dad.

"What they agree on," continued Bantam, "is that their destiny is ultimately in their hands. Deed professes belief in an 'All-knowing, All-loving, and All-powerful God,' but when you think about it these characteristics are contrary to his belief, because his belief leaves God at the mercy of the choices of his own creatures. The Reverend believes that, without the aid or permission of his own decision to choose, God cannot help him, which is why he has to believe that those who do not make the choice or accept the invitation of God, have to be dispensed with, one way or another. The Reverend and his flock believe themselves to have an exclusive hold on God that is based upon their selection of Him, which inevitably concludes in a 'devil take the hindmost' attitude toward those who do not share their choice."

"So, what you are saying," interrupted the youngster, "is that only by their believing in Him is God enabled to love them forever."

Bantam quickly affirmed Norm's observation, "Well said. Which means that their idea of God's love is not unconditional. His love, according to their way of thinking, is conditioned upon their own power and ability in their lifetime to accept it! Which wouldn't really make it unconditional love at all, now would it?

"As for Xen, he understands that we are all connected somehow and that in the end love must win out for all of us, or we are all in trouble. So, he rejects the Reverend's warnings of eternal retribution for what they are—damnable rubbish!

"Now Xen, instead of trusting in the exclusivity of a one-time decision, and/or to the adhering of it, like Deed does, trusts in the making of multitudes of decisions and choices until, without any interference from Anybody else, he eventually arrives at perfection and eternal bliss, even if the pilgrimage requires hundreds and thousands of lifetimes. Either way, Deed and Xen place their trust in, and so rely on, their decisions, on their ability to choose, which elevates and feeds the very self-importance which they both strenuously profess to deny."

Bantam, having exposed the paradox, pressed on toward the solution. "What I know, and not just because of one experience in the ring, although that sure did pop my eyes open, is that I am not in control. Everything around us says so, all of the time; however, most of us, most of the time, are so self-absorbed that we fail to see it or admit it.

"Sometimes we are rudely awakened to the fact that we do not ultimately control anything by the uninvited intrusion of tragedies, and the consequences of mistakes, both our own and others, into our lives. At other times we can be pleasantly awakened to the same truth, like when we enjoy the glory of a sunset, the first bloom of a flower, or . . ." and here Bantam could not help adding, "the stillness of a moonlit night."

After some reflection Norm agreeably asked, "I think I know what you mean, but if we aren't in control wouldn't everything be in chaos?"

"Yes, son, it would, but there is a world of difference between exercising responsibility, that is, being placed in a position of accountability or authority, and thinking you are in total control of anything—let alone everything."

The young eagle pondered for a few minutes and then with the precision of one devoid of guile he asked, "But what if we do not want to be made responsible or accountable for anything, Pa?"

"Tough luck, kid. You are not the Creator! It is His plan that is unfolding, not yours, and not mine either, and definitely not Deed's or Xen's. All I can tell you is that when you have a job to do, like it or not, you can't ignore it and you can't run away and hide from it, you simply have to do your best. And, if you are honest with yourself, you will admit that you hardly ever, if ever at all, achieve perfection in anything you do, and more often than any of us might care to admit, we fail, and sometimes we fail pretty miserably."

"So, what are we supposed to do when we realize that we have failed?" inquired Norm.

"Admit it! And when the opportunity comes around again, which it tends to do in one way or another, try again," chuckled Bantam sardonically.

"But why keep trying if all we do is keep failing?" asked Norm.

"Because what is very patiently and constantly being demonstrated, like I said, is that we are not in control, nor are we fit to be in control, but that Somebody else, who is incredibly patient, is. And that is how we learn that unconditional love is really full of mercy. We are all living proof that by ourselves, individually and collectively, try as we might, we are incapable of properly conducting our own lives or of ideally governing the lives of others. A lesson obviously lost on Garic," declared Bantam.

"Yeah, what about him? I don't think he puts any credence in Deed or Xen, does he?" interjected the young eagle.

"No, no, he doesn't, or if he does he does not believe too much in what they say. He was born to rule—or should I say, misrule, and he does a good job! He has his little world under control right now and because it serves his purpose he allows or even promotes the teachings of Deed or Xen, even if only as a distraction, but, if push comes to shove, he will happily dispense with their crazy ideas because they are only a convenience that he uses to control the coop by dividing and pitting chickens against one another."

Bantam continued by clarifying, "Garic reminds me of the bird I met in my last fight; he thinks he has this place under his feet just like that killer had me pinned by the throat. Son, it's simply ridiculous to think that any of us are in control," underscored Bantam. "We didn't start this bang-shootin' match, and we ain't going to finish it. I didn't ask for the good things in my life, and I didn't ask for the bad. I didn't ask to be in this coop. I didn't ask for Ma. I didn't ask for you and you didn't ask for me. I didn't ask to be a fighting cock. I didn't choose my parents; come to think of it, I didn't even ask to be born."

Temporarily exhausted by his own expostulation, Bantam paused and gathered himself, "Back to Garic: My guess is that he doesn't think much beyond the end of his beak because his confidence is solely in himself. Which, I was about to say, makes him more honest than Deed and Xen, but perhaps it would be more accurate to say that Garic's agenda is simply more obviously ruthless than theirs."

Bantam, correctly discerning the look on his son's face to be one of understanding, if not agreement, proceeded to explain further. "However, no matter how much Garic may or may not wrestle with his ultimate fate, if he is to maintain his dominance over the flock, he must live under the burden of thinking that he has to continually subdue and control the flock every second of every minute of every hour of every day of every month of every year. Being responsible for this coop, let alone the entire universe, is a full-time occupation, and that sure must keep him awake at night."

Then, slapping his thigh in delight at the sudden realization of a hitherto unconnected thought, Bantam cackled, "Which might explain why he never misses waking up in time to deliver his sunrise sonata!"

The humor was almost entirely lost on the distracted young eagle whose active mind had continued pondering, "But, Dad, all the mistakes that are made, how do we pay or make up for them? I mean, our mistakes cause terrific amounts of suffering to ourselves and others."

Norm's question caused Bantam to momentarily reflect that it had personally taken him a longer time to arrive at the conclusion that had so immediately troubled and just been expressed by Norm. Quickened by the strong sense of justice and earnest compassion in his son, he set about answering the demands of such an honest and tender inquiry as best he could.

"Son, what would you think if I told you that in this regard the Reverend is correct, and that the price for all the mistakes has already been paid? But, contrary to Deed's presumptuous and merciless nonsense, everything will be restored—with interest! All the hurt and suffering will one day be turned by unconditional love and limitless mercy into something that we will all share together as a gift of remembrance. Without the gift of those memories we would have no contrast and would not be able to appreciate and enjoy the bliss of a future in which we will never inflict or experience hurt or pain ever again! Remember, Somebody else made us and He did so without consulting us about how or why we were made. With each passing day I see more fully that everything that we are experiencing is teaching us thankfulness so that we will fully be able to know how to be grateful for and enjoy the goodness and peace that awaits us all."

Norm, quick to affirm the thought, leapt ahead as he recollected one of the debates that had endlessly preoccupied the loft, "So, the timeless dichotomy of good and evil—"

"Is not timeless!" interjected Bantam. "*Evil*, that is, bad things, will cease to be, once they have served their purpose in teaching us to appreciate the good things!" Then, after another slight pause Bantam, catching his train of thought, pulled the weaving of his exposition together as he continued, "Oh, and make no mistake, we will give account for our lives. One way or another everything that has been done, good and bad, has to be fully revealed for what it is, and only then can the entire universe arrive at the Final Judgment, which is, having been confronted with the truth that we are all legends in our own minds," and here Bantam paused again, " . . . we will all appreciate that God is really, really, really good. And that, my boy, is probably the greatest understatement that I will ever make!"

Norm sat very still for a minute or two while he thought through and embraced the simplicity and the enormity of what Bantam had posited until finally he gasped, "What a plan! It's so complete! It explains everything that Deed and Xen couldn't. In fact, it reconciles and exceeds the very best of what they hope for."

"Yes, and Magnus too!" laughed Bantam, the relieved laugh of someone who has finally been able to share a long-held secret, and then emphatically added, "and it's gonna happen with or without their permission, or ours for that matter! Magnus does believe there is a God who is in control, but I think that he is blinded by his mission in life. His sense of duty prevents him from recognizing that God is in total control of everything. As noble as he is, he cannot fully rest in the peace that God's love is unstoppable!"

Both birds were now lost in silent incredulity as their hearts probed and reveled in the unfathomable and delightful promise of what Bantam had shared, but Norm would not have been Norm if had not asked the final, inevitable, and unavoidable question.

"Dad, I can't help but keep from wondering—if everything that is happening is planned and under Somebody else's control, and if everything is going to turn out all right, then why should we try to do anything?"

Bantam, placing a wing on his son's shoulder, replied candidly, "Son, I haven't fully figured that one out yet," and then in a very sincere voice he added, "but there are times when I feel like I already know the answer but I just can't quite spit it out.

"One thing I am convinced of, Somebody else is working out a huge plan, and though our wills are involved they are subject and subservient to a greater Will. Our will power can't get us there—no matter how tight we clench our butts! I know because I've tried and failed, lots of times, daily! And before you ask it, no, we do not have free will, because if we did I, for one, would not be in this coop! You see if I really had free will it would mean that I would have to have absolute and total power to do anything at anytime, something I do not pretend to have but Somebody else does, and if you think about it, if we are to enjoy peace and harmony in the end, then there can only be One who does have free will, and His Will must be done, and His Will must be for love and mercy to triumph overwhelmingly, otherwise everything will remain in conflict.

"It seems we are being given every opportunity to prove that we are not capable of controlling things, or should I say, that we are not capable of perfectly controlling things, although it seems for the time being that some of us, and some more than others, are graciously being allowed the illusion that we can, by ourselves, achieve perfection. In the meantime, what I do know is that truth has a way of revealing itself, and that all I can do is live in as much peace as I can, which in this coop sometimes isn't very much peace at all, which is why I always remind you, no matter what they do, you have got to love those chickens.

"And now, though I know you might have many more questions, we've covered an awful lot of ground, and it's getting late." Although Bantam appreciated the understanding and acuity that his son had so readily just demonstrated, he knew that Norm had lots to digest, and so he continued self-deprecatingly, "Besides, I'm tired, and my head is starting to hurt with all the thinking. Son, we can talk more in the morning if you want."

"Sure, Dad," replied the youngster deferentially. Then suddenly, his heart overriding all metaphysical thoughts, he added somewhat awkwardly, "and Dad, thanks. I mean, not just for our talk tonight, but for everything."

Touched by his son's gratitude, Bantam reciprocated in the gracious way he had of downplaying those moments when he found himself or others discovered in the awkward vulnerability of love, "You're welcome, son, but you need to understand something. I am thankful too. Your life has given me more than either of us can possibly appreciate. Sleep well."

Norm had been given plenty to think about. Apart from the scope and depth of the subject matter that had been discussed he was surprised that Bantam's understanding and grasp of life extended far beyond rusticated homilies. Amazingly, his father had demonstrated a transcendent mastery over what he had hitherto considered exclusively lofty matters. *How, where, and when,* he wondered, *did his dad gain so much insight and wisdom?*

The old bird, in turn, was excited and relieved that Norm had drawn so much from him of the treasure of learning that he had gained from life, and especially through his exposure to the humans—and particularly from that peculiar crowd that used to meet in the barn every week. With the door to those experiences having been opened, he happily anticipated the sharing and exploring of his pilgrimage with such a bright and receptive heart.

Father and son, both lost in their own thoughts and enjoying that glorious sense of peace and well-being that attends and fills a soul when it is blessed with the awareness that all is well and is exactly as it should be, silently settled down. Little did they know that a good night's sleep was not to be their portion as the answers to Norm's question had been dispatched and its unwitting messenger was closing in on them very quickly.

CHAPTER ELEVEN: LOVED TO DEATH

Norm awakened to the discordant shrill of squawks ripping through the night, but before he could react Bantam had already charged out of their roost and was headed in the immediate direction of the noise and alarm.

Giving chase, the eagle arrived just in time to see Bantam disappearing through the hatch of a henhouse, which looked like it must have been pretty empty because most, if not all, of its terrified occupants were raucously charging around the coop in total panic.

Strange, frightful, and unidentifiable sounds emanated from the henhouse but they did not last long. Norm, determined to follow his dad's courageous lead, was venturing toward the open hatch when out of it exploded a tangle of feathers and fur. The youngster's first glance took in what appeared to be Bantam clinging determinedly to the nuzzle of a snarling creature while he flailed with his beak into the eyes and face of what Norm had heard talk of, but had never before seen—a fox.

With dread Norm then saw that one of Bantam's legs was not perched atop, but was seized in the mouth of the ferocious and frenzied animal. The intruder, spinning violently in the heat and confusion of battle, repeatedly tossed his head as he tried to shake his determined attacker from his snout while he simultaneously snapped murderously at Bantam with razor-sharp, bloodstained teeth.

As injured as he was, and with the conditioned instinct of a fighter, Bantam knew better than to let go. Despite the savageness of his foe he clung tenaciously to his adversary, pecking furiously, until the fox eventually succeeded in throwing him violently against the side of the henhouse. Knocked cold, or stunned, the fighting cock was now totally helpless. Then Norm, without thought or hesitation, did what he had to do, and charged with his wings outstretched and stood in the gap between the threatening advance of the fox and his dad.

Perhaps the gashed and wounded animal had taken enough punishment for one night, or maybe he recognized the forbidding shape of an attacking eagle, or maybe he had heard the screen door of the farmhouse slamming behind the farmer as he too rushed to the scene, but the fox halted his attack. With a final departing snarl at the two birds and a swift backward glance in the direction of the approaching human the fox scurried across the coop and slipped under the fence, and chased by two loads of gunshot, he disappeared into the night as suddenly as he had arrived.

Oblivious to the subsiding pandemonium of the chickens Norm raced to his father's side. Bantam was barely moving as he tried to take stock of his wounds. He had been covered in the gore of battle before, both his own and others, but this time he was saturated in dark blood that was ominously and thickly pouring from a deep wound in his side.

Bantam knew a fatal wound when he saw it, and would have quietly slipped into the embrace of what he was relieved to be discovering was a fairly painless end. But the presence of his son drew one final effort from the courageous and kindly bird. Fighting his last battle, Bantam refused to allow that bloody violence should be his son's parting remembrance of him. He was ready to go, but unbeknownst to him he was also being impelled and strengthened to take care of one last piece of unfinished business by a greater Father's heart.

Ever so slightly he lifted and turned his head and looked up into the distressed eyes of his son. "Not too pretty, huh?" he quipped, choking a little as he attempted to soften the shock that the sight of his wounds must have caused in the youngster.

Having ensured for the last time that he had gained the boy's undivided attention, Bantam was flooded with a lucid remembrance that gave him just enough fortitude to speak with a low but insistent urgency, "Listen, son," he panted. "I got the answer."

Norm, hardly in a philosophical mood, was struggling to accept the tragic nature of what was happening. Bantam was horribly mutilated, and for the first time that the young eagle could remember, his dad looked very,

very small, but the urgency of the effort that his father was expending caused the eagle to stoop and lower his head so that it almost touched Bantam's cracked and broken beak.

"In the henhouse I thought, *What am I doing here, and how did I get myself in this mess?* And right there, just at the moment that the critter attacked, the answer came—the reason we try to do anything is . . ." and gasping, he summoned the dregs of his physical strength and mental focus to communicate his final message to his son, "the reason we try," he gasped again, "the reason we try to do anything is . . . love.

"And son, . . ." Bantam sighed heavily, and if beaks could bend you would have detected what to Norm, as he strained to hear his father's words, was a weak but unmistakable smile. With his magnificent life ending Bantam departed with the whispered battle cry of a true peacemaker, "you've got to love those chickens."

The coop had collapsed into stillness. The dumbstruck flock had shuffled into a respectful ring, amplifying the silence that now enshrouded the two birds. For a few agonizingly precious moments Norm watched helplessly while, with eyes closed, Bantam took his final breaths. Left to himself who knows how long the young eagle might have stayed there, but very soon his cocoon of devastation was cracked open by the uncharacteristically soft approach of the farmer. Through thick, heavy tears the youngster watched as the man, holding a folded sack, knelt down beside Bantam's lifeless body.

Large, calloused, farm-wearied hands tenderly scooped up the limp and almost unrecognizable bundle of blood-soaked feathers and reverentially laid the fallen bird not in but upon the still-folded sackcloth. Realigning Bantam's twisted and broken wing and fractured leg the farmer could only sigh inadequately, "He was a fighter to the end."

As he turned to carry away his old friend, the farmer shared a moment that transcended the normal boundaries of creation as the eagle looked up into the man's face and thoughtfully agreed, "Yes, and he fought for something more beautiful than most of us have seen or imagined."

CHAPTER 12:
HOW TO PLUCK AN EAGLE

Long months later, Norm was missing Bantam more than ever, and though he had accepted that Bantam's death had been a merciful way for him to go, the hole in his heart still ached. He was relieved that Bantam had been spared the indignity of enduring old age and infirmity in the presence of many who would have delighted in, and happily taken advantage of, his decline. But the young bird, with each passing day, grew in the knowledge that he was not merely missing the presence of his remarkable father, but missing the presence of someone who was an even more remarkable friend.

He meditated often on what he had come to refer to as 'the Great Plan' and rested in the hope and comfort that he would see Bantam and Ma again—or what else was a heaven for? He even learned to laugh at himself, and grew in thankfulness that the Plan had even included the night of the Grand Gala and the exposing of all the self-pretentious nonsense that had led up to it.

Another measure of consolation that sustained him was the weekly visit that he received, mainly from the younger roosters that liked to hang around Magnus, but which more than occasionally included one or two of the older birds. Although their conversations usually opened with rueful and penetrating observations about the latest outrage of The Fed on the vestiges of what freedoms remained in The Foundations, they almost exclusively centered around the future of the coop. Unlike their older mentors, who necessarily fought a determined rearguard action against the machinations of the Süds, these birds exuded a hopeful idealism that appealed to the good that had not been beaten out of the young, and they were constantly discussing ways to awaken or resurrect the longing for liberty that they believed might still be lying dormant in the hearts of those who had been brainwashed by the Süds.

Whenever he heard their indefatigable optimism Norm was always encouraged to remember Bantam's admonition, "You've got to love those chickens." Marcus, Magnus's son, was especially drawn to Norm and he echoed the same thought a little more starkly, "Better to die for a cause that is destined to live, than to live for a cause that is destined to die." These younger birds, some perhaps a little too zealous, thought Norm, were prepared to endure anything, or even invite catastrophe, if it meant that The Foundations could be restored to the coop.

However, every day for Norm was accompanied, if not filled, with an inexpressible but persistent loneliness. This morning the young eagle was feeling peculiarly distracted and strangely separated from his surroundings, as though he were a reluctant or an unwelcome visitor to the day. If birds had fingers Norm would have wiggled one of them in his ears in an attempt to relieve an annoying and numbing sense of blockage that was caused by atmospheric compression. This baffling effect on his hearing had also subtly and imperceptibly distanced and dulled all his other senses so that they failed to fully alert or help him to recognize the metallic taste in the air and the eerie greenish tinge to the sky.

He felt not alarmed, but disconnected and detached, which is an understandable sensation for a bird that does not know that he is an eagle but who finds himself living in a chicken coop—but today was somehow different.

The young bird was gradually awakened out of his semi-somnambulistic trance by the irritating stinging of dust being blown into his eyes. At first it was a mere inconvenience but soon the young bird became aware that it was not only dust swirling around the coop. Small objects began to fly by him propelled by gusts which had also precipitated an intense and unusually purposeful movement in the flock as they frantically bustled and dashed around.

Dulled by the suppression of the day, and his recent days of loss and resignation, Norm had failed to notice that the chickens were running for cover, until he saw the farmer rushing around the henhouses slamming down the storm doors on the hatches which usually served as open doorways. Without a backward glance the farmer, having done his best to seal all the buildings in the farmyard, ran off, and for the first time Norm realized that he was outside in the middle of the day—alone. He was still more filled with curiosity than alarm, but the usually enjoyable sensation of the tugging of the wind had now become unpleasant, even threatening.

Leaning forward, the young eagle braced against the buffeting, and plunged his feet as deep as he could into the soil. Then he hunkered down, lowering his profile to make himself a smaller target for the loose objects that had begun to fly around the coop.

With a loud clang and without warning something substantial, he thought it might have been a watering can, slammed into the left side of his head, knocking him off his feet, sending him tumbling by the wind into the open space at the end of the coop where he had enjoyed his nighttime meditations. The sight in his left eye was somewhat blurred by blood from a head wound that he did not have the luxury of time to examine, nevertheless he felt some relief at not being surrounded by buildings as it gave him a better chance to see what may be blowing in his direction. Stung by hard pellets, Norm gripped resolutely downward with his feet which found better purchase in the bare open ground than they had on the pecked-over and broken soil and droppings that ran between the coops.

Never having experienced the phenomena of hail he was, at first, more disoriented than he was hurt by the myriad of miniscule missiles. His confusion was compounded by the fact that the sun had all but been extinguished by a thick turbulence. The wind dramatically increasing in strength was no longer merely challenging his stand; it had become an almost overwhelming force. With his claws firmly clenched, the eagle pulled his wings in as tightly as possible and lowered his body to the ground.

Chaos and noise roared all around him, and in the absence of any other ideas or options, Norm single-mindedly concentrated all of his strength into the prodigious grip which anchored his feet to the earth as he prepared to weather the unknown menace.

Then, and he would not have thought it possible, the torrents of air increased alarmingly in speed and ferocity as his ears were suddenly and painfully assaulted by the deeply resonating howl of an approaching tornado. For a short while he held fast, but the ground betrayed him as the soil below crumbled under the pressure of his own titanic grip. In a ball of feathers he was literally and violently uprooted by the wind and hurled savagely and unceremoniously into the perimeter wire of the coop.

Momentarily hanging upside-down, suspended and pinned midway up the fencing, he was fleetingly reminded of his helpless plight on the night of the gala. But he had no time to indulge in the vanity of embarrassment; he was in the grip of a destructive elemental force and only had survival in mind. Struggling mightily to refold his spread wings, which felt as though they were about to be ripped off, he strained his neck in an effort to reposition his head into a more streamlined position even as his feathers began to be stripped from his body.

Mercifully, unbeknownst to Norm, the approaching eye of the storm lessened the force of the wind that was pinning him to the fencing, and somehow he half-fought and half fell to the ground. Again he desperately began to dig in, but his determination was tempered by the knowledge that he was greatly fatigued by his previous struggles. Then, suddenly and abruptly, the wind stopped.

The relief granted as the eye of the storm passed over allowed the young eagle to sprawl, spent, and semiconscious on the ground. With his equilibrium and his senses slowly returning Norm peered through the gloom and viewed enough wreckage to make him realize that he was fortunate not to be badly hurt, or dead, but before gratitude could fill his heart he was assailed by the first blasts from the rear wall of the eye of the storm. As the pace of the wind again accelerated, the young eagle felt total vulnerability because he knew that there was not enough strength left in him to endure much more of the ordeal.

As the gusts quickened he forlornly picked a spot and set himself for whatever might be coming. One more time he hunkered down as low as possible. One more time he drove his now raw and bloodied knuckles and talons down into subterranean hope. One more time he squinted his eyes almost shut to the invisible malevolence. One more time he bowed his head to the inevitability of the abuse that was coming. The storm, as before but even more rapidly, increased in its intensity until the young eagle, totally exhausted, reached breaking point.

The accumulation of years of quiet despair, bitter disappointment, open ridicule, and hidden futility, flooded his heart with self-pity.

Overwhelmed and defeated, in complete disgust with himself and the world as he knew it, he prepared to relax his body and his grip on the earth in a final act of contemptuous resignation.

Then, at the very moment when he was about to surrender himself to the storm, when his tight, aching, and exhausted muscles were on the verge of release *IT* happened.

Unrequested, unbidden, and almost unheard a still, small voice spoke quietly and firmly into his heart, "Face the wind." It came again, this time made more distinct by repetition, a voice that spoke with such authority that its gentle command could not be dismissed or mistaken as a request, "Face the wind."

There was no hesitation, because that knowing voice offered Norm more than mere instruction. It informed him with surety that he was not, and had never been, alone. The empty abyss that had secretly gnawed in the depth of his heart was suddenly filled with a courage he had never known. There was no logic in his response to the voice, and if you have ever heard it you know that no explanation can or need be offered. All that Norm knew was that death was not going to bow him down. It was an enemy that was never to be embraced; it was an enemy that was to be resisted, to the very end.

Norm's situation was too desperate for his cry to have been described as a whoop of exaltation, but his seemingly suicidal action released a yell from the depths of his being which he screeched defiantly into the howling menace of the tornado and summoning up the last of his remaining strength and pushing up with his legs, and with the unthinking relish of abandonment, he simultaneously thrust out his wings.

The next thirty seconds catapulted Norm into a realm he had never known, the realm where he belonged, the realm for which he had been born. It might have been reflex, it might have been fear, he never quite knew, but he rigidly maintained the outstretched spread of his wings as he climbed within the huge spiral circumscribed by the tornado's winds. In an accelerating rush of sensation the young bird rocketed upward at a dizzying rate. He never would have one single, clear recollection of that amazing flight, as through the deafening pounding and the swirling darkness the young eagle ascended with his breath still held, and his eyes almost shut, until he reached the haven of quiet assurance above the storm.

CHAPTER THIRTEEN: FLIGHT PLAN

The amazement he should have felt at the scene unfolding below him was displaced by the sheer wonder that it was indeed below him! The height did not frighten him, but the fact that he was aloft did! What, and how, had this happened? Panicked with the burden of sustaining his flight the young bird flapped his wings—just like a chicken.

In a flurry of feathers and fear he plummeted back down into the storm, descending at an alarming pace until the voice came again, "Face the wind." This time, with a newfound trust, the young bird extended his wings. He quickly found himself once again ascending on the strong updrafts of the storm and very carefully he began to practice shaping and reshaping the tips of his wings. Little by little he learned to sculpt the air as he experimented with bolder movements that very gradually and carefully involved his head and then his body. Most of this, his first flying lesson, was the tentative implementation and application of what his heart instinctively and delightfully knew to do. Soon he was trusting, and then exulting, in the balance, the flow, and the feel of almost effortless soaring.

As the storm passed on beneath him his movements were no longer rewarded by the dramatic lift he had enjoyed in his initial ascent. Although staying aloft remained relatively easy, the ability to climb was now calling for subtler, albeit rudimentary, discernment of the unseen currents around him. Long minutes of experimentation and sheer delight slowly gave way to a gradual awareness that somewhere, at some time, he would have to come down, and, despite the original euphoria of flying, he also realized that he was tiring and not very far from exhaustion.

Angling himself so that he could describe a large lazy exploratory circuit, his keen eyes searched for a prospective landing site. Looking down he observed that the main henhouse and barn had suffered major damage but the other henhouses and the farmhouse were still pretty much intact.

However, returning to the chicken coop was not an option, decisively and without an ounce of doubt he concluded that at least for now a season of his life had passed. Bantam had done his job well; Norm felt nothing but compassion and, yes, love for those chickens. The young eagle also acknowledged the wisdom of a plan that extended far beyond his reckoning, a plan which had already removed Bantam and Ma from the coop, because if either one of them were still down there he could not have found the resolve to fly away. Assured that he and the coop were to each find their respective destinies he wished them well, especially Marcus and his friends.

With no knowledge to assist him Norm again had nothing but instinct to lead him as he continued in his searching orbit—until something familiar caught his eye. In the distance he spied the mountain range that he had so longingly viewed and again he felt the familiar sensation that had tugged at his heart during those secret nights in the corner of the chicken coop. As his eyes focused on the mysterious, alluring figures circling above the crags Norm involuntarily emitted the second screech of that day, and of his life, and wheeling in a large arc he soared in their direction.

The journey there was not long; in fact, it was quicker than he would have liked, for he suddenly realized, on a day full of epiphanies, that he was fast approaching a collection of birds that he knew nothing about. Insulated by the self-preoccupied assurance of youth he remained blissfully unaware of the peril of flying directly toward a flock that knew nothing about him.

Fortunately his naïve approach, tempered by his curiosity, was both obvious and cautious enough to not provoke immediate hostility from the birds. Also, forgotten by him, he still bore the wounds and the rather pathetic and bedraggled appearance inflicted by the storm, which, accompanied by the quirky clumsiness of his underdeveloped flying style, mercifully served to allay any sense of threat that the eagles might ordinarily have felt toward an intruder. Norm, in a melee of emotion, was beginning to recognize that the other birds were just like him! But the joy he would otherwise have felt was offset by the uncomfortable scrutiny he was undergoing. It was not just that his gaze was being returned with curiosity, and some alarm, he was also learning, as the chickens in the coop had learned, that making eye contact with an eagle can be unnerving.

Norm, misreading their searching looks, suddenly remembered in horror that he had blood on him. Dark memories of the coop and the ritual sacrifices came flooding back almost causing the young bird to flap his wings—just like a chicken. But by now he had learned enough about flight to hold himself, which gave him just enough time to detect, not the semi-glazed stare of frenzied killers, but the confident, if somewhat guarded, look of concern, even pity, in the eyes of some of the flock.

This exploratory exchange was interspersed with calls as the other birds remarked to one another about the visitation of the stranger. The circling introductory dance of the eagles was then disrupted by the sound of a mighty authoritative screech which was immediately followed by the presence of a mighty bird. Definitely older, bigger, and stronger than the other eagles the prodigious creature, definitely in charge, and definitely used to being in charge, soared majestically and ominously around the young eagle.

Norm, aided by the fact that his tongue was stuck to the roof of his beak, maintained an appropriate state of silence while he submitted to the imperious inspection.

Gradually the young eagle became aware that the eyes of the regal bird were transfixed on a particular area on him, but what? Then, with a sharpness of vision known only by eagles, Norm perceived that the august gaze of the magnificent bird was penetrating beneath the caked-on, wind-dried blood, and was focusing on the discordant white plumage that ran through his left wing. It was only then that the youngster noticed the same white shock of feathers running like a scar through the left wing of his examiner.

When you are an orphan there is a chasm in your heart that can only be filled by the love of someone who is prepared to pay the price to fill that breach, or by a happy reuniting with longing and loving parents. Norm, having experienced the former through Bantam and Ma, was now about to enjoy the latter.

The dear old rooster had been right: eventually the truth will reveal itself. Even as he saw a telltale tear well up in the eye of his father, Norm felt a warm and soothing stream flow from his own eyes as the dam of isolation melted from around his heart forever. Already his mind was full of inquiry, but it was displaced by a peace he had never before known and the knowledge that, at least for the moment, his questions could wait. The other eagles, who all shared the same distinctive marking on the inside of their left wing, began to gather around and encircle their brother, no longer with suspicion, but in the embrace of fellowship.

Meanwhile, with a presence filled with tenderness and compassion, the great bird joyfully flew alongside and then slightly ahead of his long-lost son leading him toward a lofty buttress on which was established a huge eagle's nest, the first that Norm had ever seen. The young eagle had come home.

"It does not yet appear what we shall be: but we know that, when He shall appear, we shall be like Him; for we shall see Him as He is." 1 John 3:2.

Now for the most liberating words that mankind can speak:
Thank you, Father.

ABOUT THE AUTHOR

There is only One Author, but He sure uses a lot of writers.

ABOUT THE WRITER

Ken Barber lives in Seattle. To find out more about him, please visit his website at ChoirOfHeretics.com.